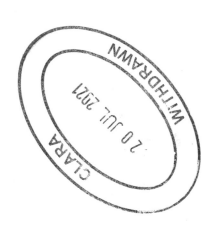

GREAT DAY for UP

By

Dr. Seuss

Pictures by
Quentin Blake

A Beginning Beginner Book

COLLINS

BRIGHT and EARLY Books for BEGINNING Beginners

Trademark of Random House Inc.
Authorised user HarperCollins*Publishers* Ltd

6 8 10 9 7

ISBN 0 00 171279 9

A Bright and Early Book for Beginning Beginners
Published by arrangement with
Random House Inc., New York, USA
First published in the UK 1975

Printed and bound in Hong Kong

UP!
UP!

The sun is getting up.

The sun gets up.

So **UP** with you!

UP!

Ear number one . . .

Ear number two.

Up, heads!

Up, whiskers!

Tails!

UP! UP!

Great day, today!
Great day
for

UP!

Up! Up!

You!
Open up
your eyes!

You worms!

You frogs!

You butterflies!

Up, whales!

Up, snails!

Up, rooster!

Hen!

Up!

Girls and women!

Boys and men!

Great day
for UP FEET!
Lefts and rights.

And **Up! Up!** Baseballs!

Footballs! Kites!

Great day
to sing
up on a wire.

UP!

Up, voices!
Louder! Higher!

Up stairs!

Up ladders!

Up on stilts!

Great
day
for up
Mt. Dill-ma-dilts.

Everybody's
doing **UP**s*!*

On bikes . . .

. . . and trees

. . . and buttercups.

UP! UP!

Waiters!

Alligators!

Up, folks!

Up in
elevators!

UP!

Up giraffes!

Great day
for seals!

Great day for UP
on ferris wheels!

UP! UP! UP!

Fill up the air.

Up, flags!
Balloons!
UP! Everywhere!

UP! UP! UP!

Great day for UP!

Wake every person,
pig and pup,
till EVERYONE
on Earth is up!

Except for me.
Please go away.
No **up**.
I'm sleeping in today.